THE WILDMEADOW HARE

For wildlife rescuers everywhere

HW

For Peta, who loves animals

DC

STRIPES PUBLISHING LIMITED
An imprint of the Little Tiger Group
1 Coda Studios, 189 Munster Road,
London SW6 6AW

Imported into the EEA by Penguin Random House Ireland,
Morrison Chambers, 32 Nassau Street, Dublin D02 YH68

A paperback original
First published in Great Britain in 2021

ISBN: 978-1-78895-323-8

A CIP catalogue record for this book is available
from the British Library.

Printed and bound in the UK.

The Forest Stewardship Council® (FSC®) is a global, not-for-profit organization
dedicated to the promotion of responsible forest management worldwide. FSC®
defines standards based on agreed principles for responsible forest stewardship
that are supported by environmental, social, and economic stakeholders.
To learn more, visit www.fsc.org

2 4 6 8 10 9 7 5 3 1

THE WILDMEADOW HARE

Holly Webb
Illustrated by Dawn Cooper

LITTLE TIGER
LONDON

1

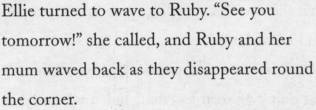

Ellie turned to wave to Ruby. "See you tomorrow!" she called, and Ruby and her mum waved back as they disappeared round the corner.

Ellie hitched up her backpack and walked on down the main road. She knew exactly where she was going – she'd been along here thousands of times – but it felt different walking all on her own. Now that Ellie was ten, she and Dad had decided she was old enough to do the journey home from school by herself. Ellie's birthday had been the week

before, and now it was the middle of March
the days were getting a lot lighter.

Ellie tried to remember all the things Dad
had said at breakfast that morning.

Don't stop and chat with people. (So she was
supposed to be rude when someone asked her
how she was? Their village was full of people
who knew her.)

Don't cross the road without looking. (There
was only one road to cross, and it was very
quiet. It really wasn't a problem.)

*Don't forget you're going home by yourself
and stand outside school for hours waiting for
me to pick you up.* (Did he really think that
was likely?)

Don't go home with Ruby without asking.
(Ruby's mum wasn't going to let her do that,
was she? Ruby's mum still picked Ruby up,

even though she was a month older than Ellie. Ruby lived a bit further out of the village, and her mum wasn't happy about her going home by herself, although Ruby had begged.)

In the end Ellie had just nodded and said yes and no in the right places. Dad had already seemed a bit uncertain and at one point she thought he'd nearly given up on the whole idea. It had helped that her sister Sophie had put down her phone for once and reminded him that she'd walked home by herself when she was in Year Five, even before she was ten. Now she had to get a bus to school, since the nearest secondary was quite a long way away.

"Ellie needs to get used to being independent," Sophie had pointed out. "Only one more year and she'll be catching the bus too. Remember all those times I missed the bus in Year Seven and you had to drive me?"

Ellie had given her big sister a grateful look. She was almost sure that Leila, her stepmum, had been about to jump in and say that maybe Ellie should wait for a bit, or something like that. She had that worried look in her eye. Ellie absolutely didn't want Leila interfering. Leila had been married to Dad for six months now, and they'd been together for a while before that, but Ellie still felt strange about her being around all the time.

She stopped to check the road really carefully before she crossed (just in case Dad had spies out). Once she was safely over, she could head on to a path across the common, and there she wouldn't have to worry about cars at all.

The common was a flat, open piece of grassland at the edge of the village. It was huge, with tiny paths criss-crossing all over, and tangles of brambles. There was a narrow road that ran through the middle of it and led to the cricket club, and there were a few benches dotted about, but most of the common was just grass. In the summer it was beautiful – a huge, wild meadow, covered in flowers. Ellie had called it that when she was little, the wildmeadow, all one word run together. It had been an Ellie-and-Mum thing.

One of the benches had Mum's name on it. It was up on the highest part of the common, where you could see for miles around, even down to the next village and the river. It had been Mum's favourite place to go for a walk, and after she died, Dad and Gran and Grandpa

had arranged for a bench to be put there. It had
Remembering Molly written along the top.

Ellie didn't often go to that bit of the
common now. Sophie went to sit on the
bench sometimes, but it made Ellie feel
strange and sad. She had only been seven
when Mum died, and there were things about
her that were hard to remember already. The
bench made Ellie feel guilty. What if she
stopped remembering at all? The Ellie who
was in the videos they had of Mum was so
small. Seven-year-old Ellie had curls and a
round sort of face. Ellie was so much taller
now, and her hair only really curled when it
was wet. Mum might not even recognize her.

Ellie had been wandering along, thinking
about Dad and Leila and Mum, and being old
enough to walk home by herself and what Mum

would have said about it. She hadn't really been looking where she was going. But then a bird darted across the path in front of her, a little black-and-white wagtail. It pulled Ellie up short – she felt as if she'd almost trodden on it. The wagtail went on hopping and bouncing up the path, as though it wasn't very worried about being almost squashed, and Ellie stopped to look properly at where she was.

She'd come further along the path than she'd realized – she was actually quite close to home. The wagtail was dotting in and out of the longer grass at the side of the path ahead of her, and Ellie watched it, smiling. Just beyond the tiny bird, a streak of brown fur suddenly shot over the grass, closely followed by another sandy-brown blur. Ellie thought

they were rabbits at first. Rabbits were all over the common – if you came out early in the morning you were sure to see them nibbling on the grass.

These were too big to be rabbits, though. They were taller and skinnier, with long legs. They looked all leg, in fact, as they bounded over the grass.

Hares! Ellie hadn't seen one in a long time, but she was sure. She was frozen still, holding her breath, but the hares didn't seem to care that she was there. They whirled over the grass, stretching out their legs in great, bounding leaps. Their ears bounced, Ellie noticed with a grin. Then the first hare turned round and stood up on its hind legs. Ellie nearly squeaked with surprise, but she managed to stay quiet. The other hare stood up too, and the pair of them batted each other with their long front paws. They looked as if they were boxing, biffing wildly at each other's noses.

Ellie stayed silently watching them for a few more moments, until they seemed to suddenly give up on the fight. They streaked away across the common in the direction of the river, leaving Ellie laughing to herself. Seeing them felt such a treat, like a special present.

The first time she remembered seeing a hare had been with her mum, sitting out on the little wooden bench that stood against the front wall of their cottage early one morning. Their door opened almost straight out on to the common, with just a track running along in front for cars – but hardly any cars came along it as it didn't go anywhere past the cottage. They could see cars or delivery vans approaching from miles away, when they did come.

Mum had often woken up early when she was ill – she'd found it hard to sleep. She liked to sit on the bench with a big mug of tea and watch the common and listen to the birds. She even sat out there when it was raining, sometimes. If Ellie woke up early, she would let herself out and curl up with Mum, half asleep. Mum would wrap her blanket around them both, and they would stare out across the grass.

Ellie walked slowly along the path, remembering Mum's hand tightening on her arm, and her breath of a whisper. "Ellie, look... Can you see, over by those brambles? It's a hare..."

Ellie had known it was special from the shake in her mum's voice. She had never seen a wild hare before, and Mum had sounded so excited. They saw hares loping across the wildmeadow a few more times that spring, and every time it felt magical.

Seeing the two hares squabbling in front of her today had brought it all back. Why had they been fighting, though? Perhaps it was a game. When Ruby's dog Chrissy had puppies, they seemed to spend half their time wrestling and fighting, but Ruby's mum had said it was all part of playing and learning how to be with other dogs.

Ellie sped up when she saw the cottage, eager to tell Dad about the hares. She unzipped the special pocket in her backpack where her door key now lived and unlocked the front door – only to find Dad lurking in the hallway.

"Were you waiting for me?"

"No! Well … I might just have noticed it was about time you got home." Dad gave her a hug. "Good day? How was the walk back? Were you really careful crossing the road?"

"*Yes*, Dad! Guess what I saw on the common!"

"Ummm. I don't know. Someone's pony straying again?"

"No! Hares! They were so funny, they were hitting each other with their front paws. You know that game where you put your hands in a pile and you keep pulling them out and piling them up? And then everyone's just waving their hands about?"

Dad was looking blank and Ellie sighed. "You must do, Dad… Anyway, they looked a bit like that."

"I haven't seen any hares boxing this year. I'll have to keep an eye out."

"Why do they do it, do you know? Are they playing?"

Dad gave her a funny look. "Um. Not quite. It's the mating season, Ellie. The girl hares get a bit fed up with being chased by the boys, so they start fighting them off. But I don't think they ever really hurt each other."

Ellie giggled. "Good for the girl hares, then."

"Exactly," said Dad, but he was looking a bit pink. "Your mum had a beautiful wildlife book with some photos of hares, I think." He hurried into the living room to look at the bookcase, and Ellie had a feeling he was trying to change the subject. "Here! You can take it upstairs if you want, but look after it, OK?"

"I will." Ellie hugged the book to her tightly, loving the thought that it had been her mum's. She hurried upstairs to lie on her bed and flick through the pages. There were huge photos of hares boxing and leaping, and even little baby hares hiding in the grass. "Leverets," Ellie murmured to herself. She hadn't known they were called that. She settled down to read the whole of the chapter, so she'd know properly what she was looking at when she saw the hares again.

She *would* see them again. She was determined.

2

Ellie checked her watch and looked anxiously down the path. It was ten past four and she was usually home by four at the latest. She could see her house though, or at least she could see its roof, just showing through the trees. It wasn't as if she was far away. Ellie turned round to gaze hopefully across the common again. She had been watching for ages, hoping to catch sight of a hare. There had been lots of birds, some bumblebees and one rabbit, but that was all she had seen.

She would wait a little bit longer. Just in

case. If she headed home, the hares would pop up again as soon as she was gone. Of course they would. That was probably what had happened yesterday. She had been so excited to see them again, that first time, and then there was nothing. Ellie turned slowly in a circle, scanning the flat grassland for leaping brown figures. Still nothing.

Except – what was that, back along the path behind her? Ellie froze, staring. Another rabbit? No, surely it was too tall and leggy to be a bunny. Rabbits looked a lot more cuddly. Hares were wild. And fascinating.

Ellie stood motionless, too excited to breathe as the hare loped slowly towards her. It didn't seem to have noticed she was there. Every so often it stopped to nibble a few mouthfuls of grass, before hopping onwards. She was so much closer this time than she had been on Monday – the boxing hares had been funny and fabulous, but they'd moved so fast, Ellie hardly had time to see them properly. She wondered if this was one of the two she'd seen.

The hare stopped eating and sat up on its back legs. Perhaps she had breathed too loudly, Ellie thought to herself, digging her fingernails into her palms. The hare was definitely checking around to see if everything was safe. Ellie could see its sides heaving with quick in-out breaths. She was close enough even to see its nose twitching. She tried to remember everything to tell Dad and Sophie later on. She wished she had a smartphone with a camera, like some of the people at school, instead of the old phone of Dad's tucked away in her backpack. It was just for emergencies, now she was walking home by herself, and it only did calls and texts, nothing else. Sophie called it a brick.

Grey-brown fur on top, a bit woolly-looking, almost curly like a sheep. Softer sandy-brown underneath. Long, long ears, with black tips. A soft, pale nose that seemed to wobble as the hare sniffed the air for the scent of danger. And the eyes! The photos in Mum's book hadn't shown how big the eyes were. Huge and amber-gold, perfectly circled with creamy fur. It was so they could see all around, the book had explained. Hares and rabbits had big round eyes on the sides of their faces to get the best view in case there were predators.

The hare had relaxed a little, and gone back to snatching mouthfuls of grass, but then there was a sudden sound from the path behind. The hare's head shot up in panic and its ears twitched wildly. Ellie looked over her shoulder and saw her dad running up the path towards her.

He didn't look happy.

"Where have you been?" he asked as he slowed down. "It's twenty past four, Ellie! I rang your phone, why didn't you answer?"

"Dad, shhh!" Ellie turned back to look at the hare – but it was gone, streaking away across the grass.

"Oh…" Dad sighed. "You were watching a hare?"

"It was so close! You frightened it off!"

"*You* frightened *me*, Ellie. You're supposed to come straight home. You ignored me calling you."

"I didn't hear it," Ellie muttered. She really hadn't, but then the phone was shoved down in one of the pockets of her backpack. "I was nearly home."

Dad shook his head. "What difference does it

make how close you are? You could have been anywhere. You had us so worried, Ellie." He waved at Leila, who was hurrying along the path towards them. "It's OK, panic over. She was watching a hare."

"Oh…" Ellie's stepmum nodded, but she looked a bit confused. "She was here all the time?"

"I'm here now," Ellie said under her breath. "I can hear you."

Dad whipped round and glared at her. "Does it really seem like the right time to be cheeky, Ellie?"

"It's OK, Pete. She's here, everything's fine." Leila smiled at Ellie. "Your dad was just worried."

Ellie tried to swallow down her disappointment. The hare had been so close, and so beautiful, and then Dad had scared it away. She knew that Leila was being nice and trying to stop Dad telling her off. But something inside Ellie hated the way she was supposed to listen to Leila. She was supposed to care what Leila thought, just because she was married to Dad now! Leila was nothing to do with her!

"He didn't need to be worried," she snapped. "It's none of your business anyway. Leave me alone!"

Ellie saw Leila's face crumple with hurt, and she felt guilty for a moment.

"OK," Dad said, his voice tired. "Home. We'll talk later, Ellie. You're making me too angry to discuss this now." Then he put his arm round Leila and said quietly, "I'm really sorry, love. Thanks for coming out to help look for her."

Ellie marched along the path in front of them, hating Dad, and Leila, and everybody. Even if the most beautiful brown hare had suddenly popped up out of the grass in front of her then, she would probably have hated it too.

Ruby was supposed to be coming home after school with Ellie the next day. Dad came very close to cancelling it, but he relented in the end. Ellie wondered if he was just too embarrassed to explain why to Ruby's mum. Ellie lost a week of pocket money, though, and Dad said she had to hang out the washing for the whole of next week. That was the household job he liked least, and he loved passing it on to Ellie or Sophie whenever they were in trouble.

Dad came to pick up Ruby and Ellie after school, but he let them walk ahead and it was almost as if they were on their own. The two girls whispered together as they walked, and once they got to the common, Ellie took off her backpack and whirled around and around, hair and coat and bag all flying.

"Come on!" she yelled to Ruby.

Ruby joined in too and the pair of them went spinning and looping down the path, until they collapsed dizzily on the grass.

"It probably means we won't see any hares," Ellie said, staring up at the deep, clear blue of the sky. "But I needed to do that."

"Me and Mum saw a hare in a field when we were driving to dancing on Tuesday," Ruby said. "I don't think I've *ever* seen them boxing, though."

Dad had caught up with them now and he was standing looking down at them, shaking his head. "Come on. Toast and Marmite."

"Ooooh, no, not Marmite." Ruby shuddered.

"Jam? Chocolate spread?"

"Chocolate spread." Ruby heaved herself up off the grass and pulled Ellie up after her.

Back at the house, Dad made platefuls of toast to keep them going until teatime, and then Ellie took Ruby up to her room to look at Mum's book, and talk. They were looking at the photos of hares when Ellie's door creaked a little and eased open, and a small ginger head peered round it hopefully.

"Hey, Biscuit… Can you smell Marmite?" Ellie said. She tore off a tiny corner of her Marmite toast and leaned over. "You can have a little bit, but that's all. Leila will tell me off if she catches me feeding you." She held out the morsel to the ginger cat, and Biscuit made happy *prrrping* noises as he galloped across the room to snatch it.

"Leila says it isn't good for Biscuit to have human food," Ellie explained to Ruby. "But he loves Marmite. The other day I went to get some juice out of the fridge and when I came back Biscuit was on the kitchen table licking my toast."

Ruby looked horrified. "You didn't eat it, did

you?" Ruby's spaniel Chrissy was the best-behaved pet Ellie had ever seen. Ellie was pretty sure that if anyone dropped a toast crust in front of her, Chrissy would helpfully catch it and hand it back again.

"No, I had to make another slice." Ellie giggled as Biscuit's rough little tongue scraped her fingers. She might not want Leila as part of the family, but she couldn't help loving her stepmum's cat. "What do you want to do now? I've got all those beads, we could make stuff. It'll be a while till tea – Dad's waiting till Sophie and Leila get home."

Ruby looked back at the book and stroked a shiny photo of a hare. "Could we go out on the common and look for them? I've never seen a hare close-up before, and you said it's the right time of year to spot them. I suppose Chrissy scares wild creatures away, so we never get to see them when we take her out for a walk."

Ellie beamed at her. She hadn't wanted to make Ruby go hare-spotting – she was the one who was desperate to see them – but luckily her friend loved animals as much as she did. "Definitely." She popped Biscuit up on her bed and added, "I'd better go and tell Dad, though. After yesterday…" She'd told Ruby about not being back on time, and how cross Dad had been with her.

"Oh yes!" Ruby nodded anxiously. "He might send me home."

"He'd never think it was your fault," Ellie promised her. Ruby was one of those people who couldn't stand getting in trouble – she and Chrissy were a very good match that way.

They went downstairs to find Ellie's dad listening to the radio and dancing while he made spaghetti bolognese. He looked horrified when he turned round and found them watching him from the doorway. "Oh! Hello, love. Hi, Ruby…"

"Is it OK if we go and sit out the front and watch for hares?" Ellie asked. "Ruby's never seen one, except from her car."

Dad nodded slowly. "Yes. Sure… Just – don't wander off, OK?"

"We won't, I promise," Ellie told him, feeling a little bit guilty that she'd scared him the day before.

"Leave the door on the latch," Dad called as they headed out. "Then you can get back in again easily. And mind the cat!"

Biscuit wasn't allowed out of the cottage – Leila had lived in a town flat before she moved in with them, and the roads had been too busy for Biscuit to go out safely. Now Leila was more worried that Biscuit would chase the birds and mice on the common, or that he might be hurt by a fox, since he wasn't used to being outdoors. The common was full of protected wild birds, and Biscuit could be a real threat. Dad had built him a little outdoor run at the back of the cottage. Biscuit could get to it through a cat flap in the side door, and it was a warm spot for him to sunbathe. Dad had even made a special cat tree for him to climb, with loads of perches and toys.

Despite all that, Biscuit still tried to shoot out of the front door every chance he got.

Ellie and Ruby curled up on the bench in front of the house, whispering to each other and looking hopefully for dark-tipped ears dancing above the grass. After a while Ellie shivered and rubbed her hands over her arms. "It's getting chilly. I'm just going to go and grab my hoodie." She dashed into the house and then came back out, zipping it up.

"Someone's coming," Ruby said, pointing to a figure walking along the path through the grass. "It's not your sister, is it?"

"Not in that hat..." Ellie peered at the tall person. "No, I don't know who it is. I don't think they're coming to the house, though. Probably just someone out for a walk." Then she glanced down in surprise as something soft brushed past her feet. "Oh no! Biscuit!" Ellie swooped to grab him, but the cat jumped sideways, looking offended, and then skittered away across the track. "He isn't allowed out. We have to catch him."

The two girls darted after Biscuit, but the cat didn't want to be caught. He seemed to think it was an excellent game – and there were bees and butterflies and exciting noises and smells outside.

"You shouldn't let that cat out here!"

Ellie turned round, shocked. A tall, elderly-looking woman was standing on the track in front of her, glaring at them, and at Biscuit. It must be the person Ruby had spotted out walking, Ellie realized. They hadn't noticed she'd come so close.

Biscuit took advantage of them being distracted and shot out further on to the common.

"Oh no..." Ellie moaned.

"This is a protected area for birds!" the woman called, just as Ellie finally managed to grab Biscuit. The little cat wriggled indignantly as Ellie walked back towards the cottage.

"We don't usually let him out on the common. It was a mistake," she said. She was hot and bothered and embarrassed, and she didn't say it very politely.

"You really need to be more careful. There are skylarks nesting out here. He's a menace to the wildlife."

"He isn't a menace!" Ellie snapped, trying to hold Biscuit still. The little cat was clawing the front of her hoodie now. "He's a good cat. I let him out by accident, it isn't Biscuit's fault. You just leave us alone!" she added. "There's no need to come round here poking your nose in!"

"Ellie!" Ruby hissed, sounding shocked.

The woman sniffed and marched away, leaving Ellie feeling ashamed of herself and angry at the same time. Hadn't she been able to see they were doing their best to catch Biscuit? Why had she been so horrible?

"You're not a menace," she whispered in Biscuit's ear. "Or maybe you are – ow!" she added as Biscuit wriggled and clawed again. Then Ellie groaned as she saw Leila's car coming down the track. "Back inside, quick!" she told Ruby.

Luckily Leila didn't seem to have noticed that Biscuit had been outside, but Ruby was quiet all through tea, and Ellie knew it was because she'd hated the scene with the woman out on the common.

"We'll probably never see her again," she whispered to her friend, as they sat watching TV after they'd eaten. "And she was mean..."

"That's the way she is," Ruby said. "She's one of those people who likes animals more than humans."

"You know her?" Ellie asked, surprised.

"She's called Mrs Bell. My mum knows her," Ruby said vaguely. "She looks after wild animals – she's got all these cages in her back garden. People call her when they find animals that have been run over, that sort of thing. She's got an ancient old bike – you must have seen her riding around the village. She lives in that blue house opposite the baker's."

"Oh…" Ellie stared at the TV without really seeing it. Dad probably knew Mrs Bell as well then, if she was local. He knew most people. Ellie wished she hadn't been rude. Not just because Dad might hear about it, but because someone who looked after injured wild animals sounded interesting. Ellie would have liked to ask Mrs Bell all sorts of things. She wondered if she'd ever had to rescue a hare. Instead Mrs Bell was going to think she was a rude little girl who didn't care about birds and wildlife at all.

3

Ellie lay in bed, wriggling this way and that. She couldn't get to sleep – she kept thinking about Ruby's shocked face, and Mrs Bell looking disapprovingly at them down her nose. If only she'd shut the front door properly when she'd gone to get her hoodie.

It was Leila's fault for having such a silly cat, Ellie thought to herself, conveniently forgetting how much she loved Biscuit. If it wasn't for Leila, she wouldn't have got into trouble.

Yes, it was all Leila's fault. Ellie yawned

and snuggled her face into her pillow, feeling much better.

Ellie had spent so much of the night convincing herself that she was right to be angry with Leila that she couldn't get rid of the thought the next morning. She marched downstairs for breakfast feeling hard done by, and flounced into a chair. She even glared at Biscuit, who was sitting innocently by the table, waiting to see if anyone was going to drop things.

"I'm just making some toast," Leila said, turning round from the counter. "Do you want some, Ellie?"

Ellie ignored her entirely.

"Ellie…" Dad leaned across the table. "Do you want toast? Leila's asking you."

"No!" Ellie snapped. She grabbed the box of

cereal from the middle of the table and didn't even look at Leila. She was waiting to get told off, but no one said anything. Sophie and Dad exchanged a glance, and Dad turned round to look apologetically at Leila.

Oddly enough, being ignored only made Ellie crosser. She shook far too much cereal into her bowl and then swamped it with milk, which was bad because she didn't like soggy cereal. She stirred it around for a bit, ate a spoonful or two, and then pushed it away.

"Ellie, you need to eat more than that," Dad pointed out gently. "You'll be starving by lunch otherwise."

"I'm not hungry."

"What's wrong?" Dad asked. "Are you feeling sick?"

"No! I'm fine." Ellie looked up irritably and scowled at Leila, who'd just sat down with her toast.

Leila smiled back at her and said, "Want some toast instead?"

"Why can't you all leave me alone?" Ellie growled.

"Did you have a fight with Ruby yesterday?" Sophie asked. "Is that why you're in such a bad mood? She was looking really down when her mum came to get her."

"She wasn't! Anyway, if she was, it was all

Biscuit's fault!" Ellie jumped up. "Your stupid cat!" she hissed at Leila, who stared at her, horrified.

"You're so rude!" Sophie shook her head disgustedly. "Just ignore her, Leila, she's woken up in a strop, that's all. Why do you have to be such a brat, Ellie?"

Leila leaned down to look under the table for the cat. "What's the matter with Biscuit? Did he scratch Ruby?"

Ellie stared at the floor, trying to think what to say. She shouldn't have mentioned Biscuit and now she was stuck. "He got out through the front door…" she mumbled. "And this woman, Mrs Bell, she shouted at us for letting Biscuit stray on the common. She was horrible."

"Oh no…" Leila sighed. "I'm sorry, Ellie."

"Don't say that, Ellie should be apologizing

to you!" Dad reached out to pat Leila's hand.
"Ellie, what did you say to Mrs Bell?"

"Nothing!"

"Uh-huh…" Sophie rolled her eyes.

"I told her to mind her own business…" Ellie
said sulkily.

"Oh great." Dad sighed. "Come on. Let's get
to school."

"But I haven't had any breakfast!"

"You had your chance," Dad said grimly. "Get
your stuff ready, we're going now."

Ellie stalked into the playground. Usually on a
Friday she'd be feeling happy, winding down to
the weekend. She liked school, but it was good
to have a break, and Miss Garnett always tried
to make Friday afternoons more relaxed, with

extra-long reading and other good things. But Ellie's Friday feeling was entirely gone.

It definitely didn't help that when Ruby spotted her across the playground, Ellie saw her face suddenly turn miserable. The seething crossness inside Ellie surged up again. What did Ruby have to be sad about? Ellie was the one who'd been told off!

Ellie walked over to Ruby. She knew she was scowling and she should stop it, but she couldn't. Something inside was pushing her on, and on.

"What are you looking like that for?" she growled.

Ruby bit her lip and stared at her, wide-eyed. "I'm … not…" she whispered.

"*Don't* start crying!" Ellie shook her head.

"Are you all right, Ellie and Ruby?" Miss Garnett walked past, holding her mug of tea – she was obviously on playground duty.

Ruby nodded, but she looked relieved, and Ellie just muttered, "Yes."

"Good. Nearly time for the bell, isn't it? I'm looking forward to carrying on with our book this afternoon, aren't you? I think we might finish it if we're lucky."

Ellie was pretty sure that Miss Garnett knew something was wrong, and she was just trying to stop them having a proper argument. A sudden wave of shame washed over her. Miss Garnett thought she was being cruel to Ruby, and the teacher was right. Ellie glanced sideways at Ruby and mouthed, "Sorry..." but Ruby wasn't looking at her.

Great. Another thing that was Leila's fault.

Ellie and Ruby made up at lunch, almost. Ellie told Ruby she really was sorry, and she explained about arguing with Dad and Leila and Sophie at breakfast, and how she'd just felt like snapping at everybody.

"I didn't mean to take it out on you," she said,

prodding at the custard on her sponge pudding.

"OK."

"Really? I know I was horrible."

"Yes, you were."

Ellie blinked. She hadn't actually expected Ruby to agree with her.

She did her best to be nice – or at least not horrible – all afternoon, but she was glad to be able to walk out of school and even more glad to get on to the common and sniff the air. Everything around her felt wide open and free, and the tight fury inside Ellie seemed to undo itself.

She was half watching out for hares or rabbits, or anything else interesting, but the other half of her was just enjoying the space and the wind blowing across the grass and whipping her hair around her face. She was utterly surprised to shake her hair out of her eyes and come face-to-face with a fox trotting out from a patch of gorse bushes. Ellie yelped in shock – they'd nearly walked into each other.

The fox looked quite shocked too, and even more so when Ellie yelled. It gave her a panicked look, obviously wondering if it should turn tail and flee into the gorse, or scoot out past her and across the common.

Ellie stumbled back a pace, trying to get out of the way. She wasn't really scared of the fox – she'd seen them quite often, nosing around the cottage and eyeing up the bins and the compost heap, and she thought they were beautiful. This fox was quite small, she reckoned, maybe one of last year's cubs. It still looked a bit fluffy round the face, and it had the most perfect white-shirt front and dark socks. It had huge ears too, as if it still needed to grow into them a bit.

It was then that Ellie realized the fox had something in its mouth. A sagging bundle of brownish fur, probably a rabbit. "Oh," she said sadly. "Oh, did you have to?"

It was stupid to talk to a fox, of course. And yes, she knew that it did "have to". The fox needed to eat, just as much as she did – but Ellie didn't usually see it happening.

The fox seemed completely bewildered now that Ellie was talking. It cast another panicked look around and then dropped its prey and shot off across the common, making for the belt of trees on the far side.

Ellie stood staring helplessly after the fleeing reddish-brown figure. And now it had left her with a dead rabbit.

"I wish you hadn't dropped it," she whispered. "Now it's just … wasted." At least before she'd known that the rabbit had died to keep the fox alive.

Perhaps she should bury it? Ellie glanced around, wondering what to do. She could go home and tell Dad what had happened, and maybe he'd let her come back with a spade. But she had a feeling he'd just tell her there was no point. How many rabbits did this happen to every day, just here on the common? Maybe another fox would come along and swipe it instead, or a hawk. Ellie knew she was being silly, it was only that the rabbit was right in front of her, limp and still, when moments ago it had been feeding, or sunning its soft fur. It seemed cruel to leave it lying there.

Just then, as Ellie was gazing at it, the rabbit moved.

4

Ellie crouched down, peering anxiously at the little rabbit. Had she imagined it? It was the slightest twitch… No, there it was again. The rabbit was definitely alive. It seemed to be struggling to move.

Ellie swallowed hard, feeling a little sick. There was a wound on its back leg, the skin was badly torn and she could see redness beneath it – she didn't want to look.

What was she going to do? When she'd thought it was dead, all she'd had to worry about was whether to bury it. Now there was

a chance she might be able to save the little
creature – and Ellie didn't know how. She
couldn't even look at the hurt leg without
feeling ill! She slid her eyes slowly sideways,
trying to make herself ready to look. Yes …
the skin was torn away and blood was seeping
out. But the bleeding was only slow and the
wound didn't seem too deep. Perhaps the
rabbit had collapsed more from shock and
fear and pain than from the wound itself.

As she watched, the dark eyes flickered open
and fixed on her in panic.

Not a rabbit, Ellie realized, her own eyes
widening. Now that she looked more closely,
she could see that the little creature's ears were
tipped with neat triangles of black. Her rabbit
was a leveret, Ellie was almost sure. It was a
baby hare.

At that moment, Ellie's doubts fell away. She had to do anything she could to get the leveret to safety. Hares brought back memories of her mother. They were special. She was going to make sure that this little one lived.

Ellie stood up again, looking around to see if there was anyone on the common who could help her. But she was all alone – the common seemed entirely empty, apart from a few birds wheeling high above.

You have to work this out by yourself, she told herself. So, she could run home and get Dad to come back with her… But what if the leveret crawled away while she was gone? It was definitely twitching a little more now; it was starting to recover. If it disappeared off into the bushes, she might never find it again.

Ellie chewed her bottom lip. She was remembering part of her mum's book, which had explained that sometimes people assumed leverets were abandoned and needed help because they found them on their own, huddled in the grass. But they weren't abandoned at all. Their mothers only met up with them once a day, soon after sunset, so the babies could suckle. The rest of the time, the little hares would hide out in the grassland, nestled in shallow dips in the ground called forms.

If she took the leveret home with her, the mother wouldn't know where it was. Maybe she ought just to leave it, Ellie thought worriedly. She might mess everything up by trying to help. But she didn't know how far the fox had carried the leveret in its mouth. The fox could have been hunting right over the other side of the common, for all Ellie knew. Leaving the leveret here by the gorse bushes and hoping it would be able to find its way back to its mother was a silly idea.

And that hurt leg… It probably wasn't very clean. A fox's mouth would be full of all sorts of grot; the wound was bound to get infected. That would be worse than quickly making a fox's dinner, Ellie thought, shivering a little. The poor little hare would be in pain from the wound, and then gradually get weaker and weaker. The hare needed a vet, or at least somebody who knew what they were doing.

Ellie wriggled out of her backpack, then took off her jacket and her school cardigan. Slowly – she was putting off the moment where she would have to touch the leveret – she slid the jacket and backpack on again. She stood there with the cardigan in her hands and the leveret panting and trembling in the grass in front of her. Mum and Dad had both always said not to chase or hurt any wild creatures. *Try not to bother them, just watch and feel grateful,* that was what Mum had told her. *Be still and quiet and you might be lucky enough to see them for a special moment.* Touching the leveret – deliberately picking it up – felt as if she was going against everything she had ever been taught.

Then she hissed through her teeth – Dad! She needed to let him know she was going to be late.

She couldn't risk a repeat of Wednesday. He'd definitely stop her walking by herself if she did it again. She grabbed the phone from her jacket pocket – she'd had to promise she'd turn it on as soon as she came out of school, and she'd keep it where she could hear it ringing – and stared down at it.

If she rang Dad now, he'd probably come and get her, but Ellie wasn't absolutely sure he'd want to save the hare. Even though she'd calmed down through the day, and then some more as she walked across the common, she was still feeling angry with Leila – and with Dad for making Leila part of her life. Ellie just couldn't trust her dad to do the right thing, not now. Perhaps she was being unfair, but Ellie thought he might say that rescuing the hare was too difficult, that it was better to leave the poor

creature to die quietly by itself and not interfere.
"It's nature's way, Ellie." She could hear him
saying it.

Ellie didn't want nature's way. She wanted to
make everything better.

So she didn't phone her dad – she texted
him instead.

Everything OK but will be a bit late xx

Ellie pressed send and looked down at the
little screen, relieved. Now Dad couldn't say she
hadn't let him know what was happening.

Well, he could. But it was better than nothing,
wasn't it?

Ellie slipped the phone back into her pocket
and twisted her cardigan nervously between her
hands. She couldn't put it off any longer now.

"I have to," she whispered to the little creature.
"I'm sorry, I know you must be so scared and

I'm only making it worse. But I have to do something. If I leave you here, you're not going to make it. I'm going to take you to someone who can help."

She crouched down and wrapped her cardigan around the tiny body of the hare, scooping it up and cradling it in her arms. It was so light – it hardly seemed to weigh anything at all. Now where was she going to take it, if home was no good? She knew she couldn't look after the leveret by herself, even if she could manage to hide it from Dad and Leila and Sophie. She needed an expert. Perhaps the vet in the village?

"Mrs Bell!" Ellie said aloud, annoyed with herself for not thinking of her sooner, and then she felt the leveret twitch with fear in her arms. "Sorry, sorry... I'm taking you to the absolute best person, I promise. Everything's going to be OK."

She set out quickly across the common again, wanting to run but holding back her steps so as not to jar the leveret in her arms. Luckily she knew exactly where she was going – she had passed the pretty blue house lots of times and always thought how nice it looked. The lovely house didn't fit very well with the tall, cross person she and Ruby had met on the common, though. Ellie didn't want to meet Mrs Bell again, but she had to.

"It doesn't matter if she's grumpy and horrible," she murmured to the leveret. "Even if she isn't nice to people, I know she loves animals. And I suppose she was right about Biscuit… Oh, I hope she doesn't tell me to go away because I was rude. She wouldn't, would she? Not if I explain you're hurt?"

Ellie hurried along the main road back into the village, past her school and most of the shops. "Please be all right," she kept whispering to the bundle in her arms. "We're nearly there, I promise. She'll know what to do, Ruby said. She looks after all sorts of wild animals. Oh, I can see it." She sped up a little, almost running as she reached the blue house. She shifted the leveret gently into the crook of one elbow and banged the door knocker.

Nothing – no sound at all from inside the blue house. Ellie waited anxiously and then banged the knocker again. "Please… Please, please, please…" she whispered. After all that worrying and running, Mrs Bell had to be there.

5

Ellie stared at the door, willing it to open, but there wasn't a sound from inside the house. Mrs Bell was out. What was she going to do now? Ellie looked up and down the road, biting hard on her lip. The vet wasn't far away – perhaps that was the best place to go? But vets had to be paid for… And Leila had said it was really expensive getting Biscuit's vaccinations done. Would they let her pay later, maybe?

Ellie looked down at the leveret, still wrapped in her cardigan. Its eyes were closed and its head was sagging. She really couldn't waste any more time. She'd have to try the vet. If they said no, she would call Dad and ask if he'd come and pay for the leveret to be treated. She ought to call Dad anyway, Ellie reminded herself. It must be nearly half past four already. Dad was probably getting into a state.

Ellie was about to head on down the street to the vet's when she noticed there was a blue-painted gate at the side of Mrs Bell's house. A gate that must lead down the side of the house to the garden. Hadn't Ruby said that Mrs Bell's garden was full of cages and pens? She looked after all the wild animals she rescued in her back garden... Ellie gazed hopefully at the gate. Of course Mrs Bell wouldn't hear her knocking on the front door if she was in the garden, would she?

There was no keyhole on the gate, just one of those old-fashioned latches. Ellie lifted the latch and shoved at the gate with her hip – it creaked open. Ellie peered round it, and then edged slowly into the passageway down the side of the house. She was half expecting Mrs Bell to pop out and tell her off, but the garden seemed to be empty too. Ellie nearly turned back to go to the vet's after all, but the garden was just too fascinating to leave.

It wasn't like any garden Ellie had seen before. There was a patch of straggly, untidy grass in the middle, but there were no flower beds or pots – the entire long, narrow garden was filled with sheds and pens and shelters.

Some of them looked like the sort of hutch
that a guinea pig or a rabbit might have,
which wasn't so unusual to find in a garden,
but there were several much bigger enclosures
that looked a bit like Biscuit's "catio", except
some of these had a little shed in them
too. Ellie went to peer into the nearest one,
fascinated. Looking shyly back at her from
round the door of the shed was a pointed,
golden-brown face.

"A deer!" Ellie whispered, amazed, and
the fawn stepped out into the pen to see
her properly, its delicate legs splayed a little
sideways. It looked very young, Ellie thought.
"Oh, this is perfect," she murmured to the
leveret. "Mrs Bell will definitely know what to
do. You've got to be easier to look after than
a deer. This is like a zoo."

Ellie wondered what was in the other pens, but she was a bit worried about frightening the creatures – and she needed to find Mrs Bell to look at the leveret, and soon. She shifted the cardigan and looked down at it anxiously. The little creature seemed very still.

"Mrs Bell must be out," Ellie muttered. "Perhaps I should go and knock next door. Maybe they have her number? Oh, please don't die," she added, gently stroking the leveret through her cardigan. "Not now. We're here, Mrs Bell's going to look after you. Just hold on a little bit longer."

"What are you doing?" a sharp voice demanded, and Ellie spun round in shock. Mrs Bell was standing at the end of the passage, looking surprised and rather cross. She obviously recognized Ellie from the day before.

Her frown deepened, and she added, "Oh … the girl with the cat."

"I'm really sorry I was rude yesterday," Ellie burst out. "I – I shouldn't have said you were poking your nose in. You were right. Biscuit got out by accident but we ought to have been more careful." Ellie held out the sad little bundle in her arms. "Please can you help?"

"What is it?" Mrs Bell asked suspiciously. Ellie wondered for a moment if she thought it was some nasty joke.

"It's a hare – a leveret – at least I think it is."

Mrs Bell sighed wearily. "You should have left it where you found it! It's not an orphan, the mother would have come back to feed it later this evening. How long ago did you take it? Can you remember exactly where you got it from? We might be able to re-release it."

"I didn't take it out of its form," Ellie assured her. She went closer, lifting the side of her cardigan to show Mrs Bell the little hare's leg. "I promise I didn't! I know you shouldn't ever move them. A fox dropped it, right in front of me! And it's been bitten, look. It's bleeding and I didn't know what was best. I think it might need stitches, and maybe antibiotics. My friend Ruby said you look after wild animals, and I didn't know who else to ask."

Mrs Bell nodded, and gently took the bundle out of Ellie's arms. "Yes, all right, that's different then. Let's have a look at you, little one." She sucked her teeth thoughtfully as she examined the wounded leg. "You're right. That definitely needs stitching up. We'd better take him round to the vet's."

"Him?" Ellie asked. "Can you tell it's a him?"

"I'm pretty sure, yes. I suppose you want to come too?"

Ellie blinked. She hadn't really thought this far – she had been focused on finding someone who could help. But she certainly didn't want to head off home now, without knowing that the leveret was going to be OK.

"Yes please," she told Mrs Bell eagerly. Then she remembered something, and swallowed worriedly. "Will it be expensive? I haven't got any money with me."

Mrs Bell looked down at her, and for the first time her face seemed to lighten. She smiled a little. "Don't worry. I have an arrangement with the vet – I pay when I can, basically, and they also give me a special rate. A lot of the fundraising I do is just to cover vet bills. That and food."

Ellie nodded, looking around at the pens. She could see that it must cost a lot to feed and care for all these animals.

Mrs Bell went to the back door of the house, beckoning Ellie to follow her. "We'll find a carrier for him," she explained. "Come on through here."

The kitchen table was covered with food dishes, and there were feeding bottles drying on the draining board. There was a large cardboard box on the table too, and it was definitely rustling. Ellie was desperate to know what was in it, but they hurried past too quickly. Mrs Bell led her into a small room off the kitchen, piled up with different boxes and hutches and all sorts of equipment.

"Can you reach down that carrier?" Mrs Bell pointed to a plastic and wire box up on a shelf. "We don't want anything too big, and that one's meant for rabbits. Hopefully it shouldn't smell too strange to him – he'd be terrified if we put him in a box that I'd used for a fox cub, or a cat, do you see what I mean?"

Ellie nodded. She hadn't thought about smells, but it made sense. She lifted down the box and fiddled with the clips to lift the top part up. The box worked the same way as Biscuit's cat carrier; she'd seen Leila do it before. The bundle of cardigan and hare looked worryingly small when Mrs Bell laid it inside, and the leveret didn't seem to be moving at all. Ellie couldn't even see him breathing.

"Do you think the vet will be able to help?"
she asked Mrs Bell, as they fixed the lid back
on and headed for the front door.

Mrs Bell looked down at the carrier and
sighed. "Hares are very tricky to look after,"
she explained slowly. "They seem very fragile,
somehow. They don't adapt well to being in a

shelter. But we can hope. Come on. The sooner we can get him to the vet's, the better."

The surgery was further down the village high street — it looked just like any other shop, with a big, glass window and, inside, a line of chairs for people to sit with their animals. Usually Ellie would have hoped for cats or dogs that she could look at while their owners waited, but today she was glad that the chairs were all empty. If the leveret would be upset by a box that smelled of cats, a real cat would be awful.

Mrs Bell put the carrier down on the reception desk, and smiled at the young man in green scrubs who was sitting at a computer. He sat up and peered curiously into the carrier.

"Hello, Alex. It's a leveret," Mrs Bell explained. "Only a couple of weeks old, I think. He's been mauled by a fox and he's got a nasty cut on his leg that needs stitching."

The young man made a face and Mrs Bell sighed. "I know, but maybe we can rear him if we're lucky. Has Sally got time to stitch up his leg now?"

"I'll check with her." Alex disappeared through a door behind the desk and came back with the vet, Sally, who picked up the carrier and glanced curiously at Ellie. "I'll take him through and have a look. Is this your granddaughter, Sheila?"

Mrs Bell blinked at Ellie, and looked embarrassed. "No – this is the girl who found the hare. I didn't ask your name…"

Alex laughed. "Typical. You were concentrating on the animals instead."

"I was too," Ellie said shyly. "I'm Ellie."

"Were you on your way home from school when you found him?" Sally asked, and Ellie nodded. "Do your parents know where you are?"

Mrs Bell gave Ellie a horrified look, as though she was only just noticing her properly. She hadn't thought about her age, or where she ought to be, Ellie realized. She really had only been worrying about the hare. She liked Mrs Bell more for that.

"Um. Sort of," she explained. "I did text to say I was going to be a little bit late."

"You can use our phone to call them if you need to," Sally said. "I'll go and check him out." She disappeared into the surgery, leaving Alex and Mrs Bell eyeing Ellie.

"I'll call my dad," Ellie said, pulling out her phone and flinching at all the missed call alerts on the screen. She hadn't noticed it buzzing. Maybe she needed to turn the ringer up – or perhaps she'd just been too worried about the leveret to notice. Her holding text message had clearly not been enough. Dad was going to be furious.

"Ellie!" Dad exploded as he picked up the call. Ellie could see Mrs Bell and Alex flinch slightly – they could obviously hear him too. "Where are you? What are you doing? Are you all right?"

"I'm at the vet's," Ellie tried to explain, but

Dad was still going.

"We were so worried about you! What was that message supposed to mean? You can't just send a message like that and disappear, Ellie, that doesn't count as keeping in touch!"

"It was an emergency!" Ellie yelled down the phone. "I had to! You would have done the same, Dad, honestly!"

Would he? Ellie wasn't actually sure. But she knew her mum would have done.

6

Ellie's dad arrived at the vet's about twenty minutes later. Ellie could tell that he wanted to bang the door open and stomp in and yell, but he was making himself stay calm. Dad was better at not yelling than she was.

"What are you doing here?" he said quietly, glancing around at Mrs Bell and Alex, and a woman who had just come in with a Yorkshire Terrier and was pretending not to listen to what was going on.

"Ellie rescued a leveret," Mrs Bell said hurriedly. "She was very quick-witted, she brought the poor little thing to me for help."

Ellie gave Mrs Bell a surprised, grateful look. She hadn't expected Mrs Bell to stick up for her.

Ellie's dad nodded, but he still looked grim. "That's good to hear – but she should have called. We would have brought the leveret down here ourselves, or gone to you for advice. I know you're the person to speak to about injured wild creatures."

"I wasn't sure you would," Ellie muttered.

"What?" Dad swung round to look at her.

"I didn't know if you'd do anything!" Ellie said loudly. "I thought you might just say to leave him."

Dad looked shocked, and then uncomfortable. "Of course I would have done something…"

"Even if it was really expensive to have him stitched up?" Ellie demanded.

"Yes – well – I suppose it would depend…"

"You'd have left him there!" Ellie cried, not caring that the woman with the dog was now obviously listening, her head whipping between Ellie and her dad.

"Ellie," Mrs Bell said gently. "Sometimes it just isn't sensible to try and save an animal – if they've been run over, maybe, and they're in a very bad way. Your dad's not being cruel."

"It feels like it," Ellie muttered. She glanced at Dad, wondering if he was getting really angry with her. Instead, his face looked odd. Odd but familiar. Ellie blinked at him, trying to remember when she'd seen him look like that before.

And then she remembered – it was after Mum had died, when he was still wandering around the house just picking things up and putting them down again, and not eating unless Sophie made him. He looked breathless, as though someone had pushed all the air out of him.

Ellie felt sorry – she hadn't wanted to make

him look like that. But it was still true. She
had been scared he wouldn't let her help. She
still was.

Ellie and her dad both turned as a
movement from behind the reception desk
caught their eyes – the surgery door swung
open, and Sally backed out with the leveret's
carrier in her arms.

"How is he?" Ellie gasped, hurrying to lean
over the desk.

"Mmm, he's OK." Sally sounded a bit
doubtful, Ellie thought. "I sedated him
to stitch up the cut, and I've given him
antibiotics to help. The cut should heal
fine, but it's more about the shock, to be
honest. Hares don't deal well with shock."
She smiled sadly at Mrs Bell. "You're going
to have a time of it, rearing him. Sorry."

She put the carrier down on the desk and glanced round Mrs Bell to the woman with the Yorkshire Terrier. "Sorry to keep you waiting. Do you want to bring Billy through?"

When they'd both gone, Ellie, Mrs Bell, Dad and Alex all stared at the carrier. Sally had left Ellie's school cardigan in there as a soft bed for the leveret, but he wasn't wrapped up in it now.

He lay slumped on the navy fabric, his tawny-brown fur ruffled. He looked very small, and very fragile.

"Are you going to take him home now?" Ellie asked sadly. "Where will you put him? Have you got an empty run?"

"Yes, I've got the space," Mrs Bell said slowly. "That isn't the problem."

Ellie looked up at her in surprise, and then remembered what Mrs Bell had said about vet bills being the most expensive bit of caring for her wild creatures. "Oh! Is it the money? I can give you some. I've got birthday money saved up, and I don't know what I was going to use it for anyway."

Mrs Bell smiled at her. "Money's always a problem, but that isn't what I meant. Sally's right – hares are really hard to rear. They're just – fussy, I suppose. They're incredibly nervous. You've seen them in the wild, haven't you, out on the common? The way they never sit still. They're constantly up on their haunches, looking around, checking to make sure nothing's after them. They're prey animals, that's why. It means they find it really stressful being around other creatures. I've got two fox cubs in my garden at the moment – one had been hit by a car, and the other one got caught in a trap."

"Oh…" Ellie looked down at the leveret anxiously. He wasn't going to like that. *She* wouldn't want to be kept somewhere close to the same kind of animal that had mauled her leg.

"Exactly." Mrs Bell heaved a sigh – but Ellie thought it sounded just a little bit overdone. As if she was putting it on… "Hares actually do much better if they're looked after somewhere on their own.

Where they're the only creature being cared for."

Ellie's eyes widened, and she glanced round at her dad. Dad was checking his phone – probably for messages from Leila – and it took him a moment to work out what was going on.

"Oh, now hang on…" He looked up, his face horrified. "You're not serious!"

"Dad, please!"

"Ellie, we don't know the first thing about looking after wild animals! The vet and Mrs Bell just said how difficult hares are to rear – we wouldn't know where to begin!"

"But we won't be doing it on our own," Ellie told him pleadingly. "Mrs Bell can tell us exactly what to do." She turned back, looking at Mrs Bell hopefully. "You could, couldn't you?"

"Of course. And I can lend you all the

equipment you'll need – the milk powder, everything. I just don't have a safe space to rear him myself." Mrs Bell looked at Ellie's dad and sighed. "I know it seems a bit strange, suggesting that Ellie takes this on – I can try and find a shelter that will take him, but they're all going to have the same problems that I do – they're full. And busy! Hares hate that. They always do best one on one, somewhere really quiet. A shelter full of different animals just doesn't work for them at all."

Dad nodded. "Well, yes, I can see that, of course. But how can Ellie rear a baby hare when she's supposed to be at school? No, I'm sorry, Ellie, it's impossible."

Ellie felt her shoulders sag. Of course, she hadn't thought of that. Probably the leveret would need feeding lots of times through the

day and the night. Even if she could persuade
Dad to let her get up to do night-time feeds,
there was no way she could miss school – and
now didn't seem to be the time to ask her dad if
he could feed the leveret instead.

"Actually, I'm sure this leveret is old enough
to manage on two feeds a day," Mrs Bell said,
eyeing the limp brown form in the carrier. "He's
at least a couple of weeks old. So you could feed
him when you get up in the morning, and then
in the evening, about seven or so."

"Oh!" Ellie nodded eagerly, and then looked at Dad, her face full of hope.

"But if you do decide to take this on," Mrs Bell added, "it would be much better if it was only you feeding him, Ellie. We want to be able to release him back into the wild as soon as he's able to manage by himself. If he gets used to humans, that's not going to help him." She made a face. "He needs to stay wild and shy, do you see what I mean?"

"Yes," Ellie said thoughtfully. "I suppose if he got really tame he might start going up to people on the common — dogs would be able to catch him."

"Exactly." Mrs Bell looked at her approvingly and Ellie felt herself go pink. It was so nice that Mrs Bell didn't think she was that silly, bad-tempered girl who couldn't look after her cat any more.

Then Ellie's face fell suddenly. "But what about Biscuit! That's our cat, the one you saw me with. The leveret would be able to smell him, wouldn't he? Oh no…"

Mrs Bell looked thoughtful. "Didn't you say Biscuit was an indoor cat? He was only outside by mistake, wasn't he?"

"Yes. He stays indoors, but Dad built him a catio round the side of the cottage," Ellie explained. "It's like his own little outdoor space."

"That's very sensible." Mrs Bell smiled at Ellie's dad, and Ellie's dad looked back suspiciously, as though he didn't like where this conversation was going. "You probably wouldn't want to keep a leveret in the house anyway," Mrs Bell explained. "It would be too noisy for them, and too many people around. So Biscuit wouldn't be a problem, if you had space in a shed, maybe?"

"The summerhouse! We have a summerhouse at the end of the garden!" Ellie burst out. "Nobody uses it much – it's always a bit spidery, but I wouldn't mind. We could keep him in there."

"Now hang on…" Dad shook his head. "This is all going a bit fast. I still don't think it's a good idea."

Ellie took a deep breath, to stop herself from snapping back at Dad. It was what she always did. But now, with Alex and Mrs Bell there too, it was easier to keep calm. Not being at home helped too – the vet's was a space that didn't belong to her and Dad. They didn't have a way that arguments always went, here.

"Why not, Dad?" she asked, deliberately keeping her voice calm, and slow.

"Well, because – because you're too young." Dad shook his head firmly. "I'm sorry," he added to Mrs Bell, "but you've already said that hares are really hard work. Ellie's only ten. She's not responsible enough to care for a tricky wild creature. She's proved that today, running off like she did. You'd be much better off finding another shelter to take the leveret. We can't help you."

Ellie felt tears burning behind her eyes. Was that really what Dad thought of her? That she wasn't responsible?

"Of course Ellie should have let you know what was going on sooner," Mrs Bell said gently. "But she did text you. And you must see that she had good reason to be out of touch. I'd hardly call rescuing a wild creature running off. Ellie was dealing with an emergency, she had to stay calm and make a very quick decision. You should be proud of her."

Ellie swallowed hard. Mrs Bell was being so nice, but now she felt even more like crying. She supposed what Mrs Bell was saying was true, but it hadn't felt like that at the time. She'd felt dithery and desperate and frightened.

Dad opened his mouth and shut it again, glancing helplessly at Ellie. "Look," he said at last. "You don't understand. Ellie's mum…" He stopped, blinking worriedly. "Ellie, sweetheart, I don't want to talk about this in front of you."

"I'd like it more if you did," she whispered.

"I don't like it when you talk about me when I'm not there."

Her dad sighed and reached out to take her hand. Ellie hesitated for a moment, and then folded her fingers in his. Both their hands felt very cold. "All right. I suppose it's better that you understand. I'm worried about you, Ellie. Mrs Bell keeps saying how difficult this is going to be – but have you thought about what that actually means?"

Ellie frowned at him uncertainly. "Um. I suppose…"

"If you can't get the leveret to feed, or he gets upset because he can smell Biscuit, or one of a hundred other things goes wrong, he's going to die." Her dad's hand tightened on hers, and he looked down at the floor. "I'm not sure you're ready for that. Not after your mum…"

"But … that's like saying I'm not allowed to be upset about anything ever again," Ellie pointed out, her voice shaking. "Dad, you can't make that happen. It's not – it's not *real*."

Her dad didn't say anything. He kept on staring at the floor, and then after a moment, he pulled at her hand, just a bit. Ellie heaved a huge sigh and hugged him tight around the middle.

"All right," he muttered. "OK. Let's do it."

7

Ellie was going home with the leveret's carrier on her lap. It was hard to believe that it was actually happening – that Dad had said yes.

I'm going to hand rear a wild hare, Ellie kept telling herself.

Because she *was* going to manage it, even though Mrs Bell and Dad and Alex at the surgery kept warning her how difficult it was going to be. Ellie was determined. She couldn't let the little hare go.

Dad had driven her round to Mrs Bell's to pick up all the equipment they needed

– a cage to house the leveret, a little run to put him in out in the garden, and a tub of special milk powder to make up his feeds. And a great big bag of hay. It was all squashed into the back of the car as they bumped gently along the track across the common. Ellie had several pages of notes from Mrs Bell too, all about how much to feed the leveret, and when, and what he should weigh.

As they pulled up at the side of the house, Leila and Sophie flung open the side door.

"What's going on?" Sophie demanded. "What were you at the vet's for? Leila said there was a hare, it didn't make sense."

Dad sighed and lifted the cage out of the boot. "No. It doesn't make sense. We've adopted a wild leveret. Blame Mrs Bell."

"Mrs Bell?" Leila exclaimed. "That woman who runs an animal shelter out of her back garden? Why is she giving us leverets? We don't know anything about leverets! Pete, are you sure this is a good idea?"

"Nope." Dad sighed. "I'm pretty sure it isn't. Like I said, blame Mrs Bell. And Ellie. But actually, we don't have to do very much – it's Ellie who's going to be in charge. And the leveret is going to be in the summerhouse in the garden."

"Ellie…" Sophie rolled her eyes. "Ellie, what have you got yourself into?"

"I couldn't leave him, Soph," Ellie said, her voice suddenly shaking with tiredness. It seemed a very long time since the fox had popped out in front of her. "A fox was going to eat him. He's had stitches and everything.

He must be so scared."

"Oh wow…" Sophie murmured, coming to peer in through the wire part of the carrier. "He's so little. Are you sure that's not a rabbit?"

"No, Mrs Bell and the vet said he was a hare. But he's only a couple of weeks old. He's got black ear-tips, look. That means he's a hare."

"Come on, Ellie," Dad said. "Let's go and put this stuff in the summerhouse. I'll help you move the garden chairs out of the way. And I'll get the spiders out of there as well."

Ellie smiled at him. Dad sounded tired too, she thought. It must have been hard for him, talking about Mum to Mrs Bell.

The summerhouse was full of spiders, and there were great grey hanks of webs all over the garden furniture and other clutter that had ended up in there. Dad took out three enormous spiders – ones that were so big, Ellie was certain she could tell they were cross about being moved. They waved their legs about peevishly and Ellie clung on to the carrier, her heart racing and her fingers feeling colder than ever.

"There." Dad came back from the far end of the garden. "It's going to take them weeks to get back from all the way over there. I promise, Ellie. You're safe."

"Thanks," Ellie said shakily.

The summerhouse was a bit like a posh garden shed, with double doors at the front, and windows. Nobody in the family went in there very much. Sophie had talked about using it to do painting in for her Art GCSE, maybe, but she hadn't got around to it yet. It was the perfect place for keeping the leveret's cage.

"It doesn't look very big," Dad murmured, as he lifted the cage in and set it down on the floor. "Not when you think of the size of a hare and those long legs."

"Dad, look," Ellie whispered. "He's moving!"

In the carrier, the leveret's eyes were open and his soft nose was twitching. He wriggled a little, cautiously watching Ellie and Dad. He looked terrified, Ellie thought. The sooner they could leave him to settle down in his quiet cage, the better.

"Mrs Bell said the small cage is fine for the first couple of weeks," Ellie whispered to Dad. "Then she's going to bring us round a bigger one. By the time he's nearly ready to go back in the wild, he's going to need a really big sort of hutch thing, but Mrs Bell said she's got one of those. She's lent it to somebody who rescued some chickens and didn't have anywhere to keep them. But she's going to get it back."

"And this really big hutch goes where?" Dad asked, looking around the summerhouse.

There wasn't a lot of room, with the two of them and the chairs and the cage.

Ellie looked meaningfully at the lawn, and Dad sighed. "That hare had better not eat my tulips." But he didn't sound very serious and Ellie grinned at him.

"I'll have to check the list. I don't think he's allowed tulips. But they do like dandelions. You're always moaning about dandelions in the lawn…"

Dad put his arm round her shoulders, and pressed his nose into her hair. "Sometimes you really remind me of your mum."

They were silent for a moment and then Ellie pulled away. "We'd better get him in the cage, Dad. I've got to line it with newspaper and hay, and then – I suppose I have to put him in it. I can leave him to get used to it while I go and mix up the milk for his feed."

"Newspapers are here, look." Dad passed her a bundle. "I got them out of the recycling."

Ellie opened the cage and laid a layer of newspaper over the bottom. She covered it with a thick layer of sweet-smelling hay. There were even tiny, dried clover flowers in it, and it looked like beautiful stuff to sleep on.

"I'm nervous," she said, looking up at Dad. "I know I carried him all the way to Mrs Bell's, but it feels different, reaching in and taking him out of the carrier."

"I know what you mean," Dad agreed. "Hang on. Let's shut these doors, just in case – I really don't want to be chasing an escaped hare round the garden."

Ellie giggled, but it didn't feel very funny. Suddenly, she wished she'd asked Mrs Bell to come back with them and help. She watched Dad close the doors and then she unclipped the top of the carrier, easing it open slowly in case the leveret made a wild leap for freedom.

He didn't. He didn't do anything. He just sat in the open base of the carrier, trembling, as though Ellie and Dad were the scariest things he'd ever seen.

We probably are, Ellie realized. Unless … perhaps the fox had been worse. But at least the leveret would know what a fox was. Humans must be completely strange and terrifying.

Ellie reached inside and lifted him out

of the carrier, scooping him up with her cardigan still half wrapped around him. She didn't want to take it away — it must feel at least a little bit familiar to him by now. And she did have another one for Monday.

She laid the hare in the cage and quickly

fastened the top back on. She'd hoped that once he saw that he had more space to move around he might start to hop about and explore, but he still crouched, frozen and trembling, on her cardigan.

"It's OK," Ellie whispered, looking up worriedly at Dad. "You're safe." She sighed. "I'll go and mix up the milk for him."

Dad nodded. "I'll come and start making tea for us too," he said, as they shut the summerhouse doors behind them.

Ellie blinked. She'd forgotten she hadn't eaten anything – she was usually really hungry after school, but she'd been too busy to think about it.

Mrs Bell had given them a big syringe to use for feeding the leveret – she said they were easier to use than bottles, especially at first, because the leveret probably wouldn't understand what she was trying to do, and wouldn't know he had to suck on a bottle. There seemed to be so much to remember – sterilizing everything, boiling the water to

mix up the milk, even weighing the leveret
to work out how much to feed him.

"Um, Dad? Can I borrow your kitchen
scales?" Ellie asked hopefully.

"There's a scoop to measure the milk, Ellie,
you don't need to weigh it," Dad pointed
out.

"I have to weigh *him*," Ellie explained.
"Mrs Bell gave me this sheet, look. It's a list
of weights and how much milk they ought
to have when they weigh that much. She
thought he was a couple of weeks old, so I'm
making forty millilitres of milk – if it's too
much I'll just squirt some out before I start
feeding him."

"You are not weighing a hare in that
bowl," Dad muttered, looking at the nice
metal bowl that came with the scales. "You

can have one of those ice-cream tubs in the cupboard. You'd better write 'Hares Only' on it, or something. Oh, and I found you the camping lantern, look. It's getting dark and soon you won't be able to see what you're doing out in the summerhouse."

Ellie loaded herself up with the lantern and the scales, and a bowl with the syringe of warm milk, and marched determinedly back to the summerhouse. She had a towel to wrap the leveret in as well – Mrs Bell's notes said that feeding could be messy until the baby animals had got some practice in.

The leveret was still hunched up inside her cardigan – it looked as though he hadn't moved at all, and Ellie chewed her lip anxiously. Surely he ought to be looking around his new home, having a good sniff and explore?

"Are you still too scared to move?" she whispered to him, as she put the scales and the ice-cream tub on the little garden table. "It's OK, I promise. We only want to help." Trying to move as slowly and gently as she could, Ellie took off the top of the cage. Then she lifted the leveret out in her cardigan and sat down with him in one of the garden chairs. "You have to let go of this for a minute," she explained, carefully tugging the cardigan away from his paws. "I can't weigh you wrapped up in a cardigan, can I?"

The leveret felt tense and rigid as she lifted him into the ice-cream tub, and Ellie sighed. "Well, at least Mrs Bell was right about you being two weeks old. A hundred and twenty grams – that matches the chart exactly. And it means I've done you the right amount of milk too. I bet you're hungry. This stuff smells nice, doesn't it?" She stopped, and swallowed. "I'm chattering because I'm nervous," she explained to the leveret as she put him back on her lap and wrapped the cardigan around him. "I've never done this before." She picked up the syringe and looked at the little creature hopefully. Surely he could smell the milk – perhaps he'd brighten up and want to have some?

"Next to your teeth," she murmured, looking at the instruction sheet. "OK." She pressed the end of the syringe gently against the leveret's mouth, trying to push it in beside his teeth. The little hare didn't seem to react – but his mouth was clamped tightly shut and Ellie couldn't get the syringe in at all. "Hey," she whispered. "Don't you want it?" She squeezed out a little bit of milk, so that it dripped on to the leveret's fur, but he didn't even try to lick it off. It just dribbled down his chin, soaking the fur on his neck.

"I can't make you drink it," Ellie said, sitting back and gazing at him. "You have to try just a little bit. Please?" She sighed. Mrs Bell had said that it might take a couple of days for him to get used to the idea, but Ellie had so hoped he'd want to eat straight away. He was so small, and he looked so thin. Could he really last a couple of days without eating? "I suppose I'll try again tomorrow morning," she murmured, putting the syringe down. "Let's put you back in your cage, OK? You can have a sleep and you'll be hungry in the morning, won't you?"

It seemed mean to leave the little hare all on his own for the night, but Ellie didn't know what else to do. She could sleep in the summerhouse next to him, perhaps, but would that help? He was so scared of everything, she might just make things worse.

Ellie slipped him back into the cage, and watched him huddle down, only his nose and whiskers moving at all.

What if the leveret had simply given up?

8

The next morning, Ellie dashed out into the garden in her pyjamas as soon as she woke up. She couldn't wait. What if the leveret really had given up? It was horribly possible that he'd just faded away and died overnight.

But he was still there, aware and gazing back at her with those huge amber eyes. They were circled with pale golden fur, and they stood out against his tawny-brown coat.

"Hello," Ellie whispered joyfully. "Are you hungry yet? You must be starving. I'll go and mix up some milk for you. It'll be a little while, though. I've got to boil the water for the milk and then let it cool down. I'll be as quick as I can." She ran back up the garden, her bare feet slopping around in her wellies. The house was Saturday-morning quiet – no one else was up, and they probably wouldn't be for a while. Biscuit wandered into the kitchen and rubbed himself against Ellie's legs, purring loudly.

"OK, I'll feed you too," Ellie said, leaning down to stroke him – but then at the last minute she pulled away, remembering what Mrs Bell had said about hares being able to smell cats and dogs and foxes. "Oh! Sorry, Biscuit. I can't stroke you – not when I'm about to feed the leveret, in case he smells you." She got the cat food bag out of the cupboard and filled Biscuit's bowl. "There you are, though."

She hurried back to the summerhouse with the syringe and her towel, and opened up the cage ready to try feeding the leveret again. Her heart sank as he stayed stiff and terrified on her lap – and again when she tried to get him to feed. The syringe just wouldn't go into his mouth.

"Please..." Ellie whispered. "You'll starve if you don't eat. You've got to." Was it her imagination, or did those huge eyes look slightly sunken already? "You haven't had *anything*. You can't go on like this."

She sighed wearily and ran her hand over

the little hare's soft coat. "What am I going to do?" she murmured. "Please don't give up."

After a few more tries, Ellie laid the syringe aside and slipped the leveret back into the cage. It wasn't working and there was no way she could make him drink. Miserably, she shut the summerhouse doors behind her and trailed back up the garden to the house. In the kitchen, Ellie slumped down at the table, staring at the useless syringe of milk. She swallowed, and swallowed again, trying not to cry, but she couldn't stop herself. What if the leveret never ate anything? What if it had all been for nothing and he died?

Ellie laid her head on her arms, trying to hold back any noise. She didn't want to wake anyone up. Her shoulders heaved and she could feel tears soaking into the sleeves of her pyjamas.

"Ellie! Hey, Ellie, what's wrong? Oh, don't cry, sweetie." Someone was crouching down beside her, stroking her hair – and for a tiny, weird moment, Ellie thought it was her mum. She looked up, confused, and saw Leila staring at her anxiously.

"What's the matter, Ellie? Is it the leveret? Oh – he's not…"

Ellie shook her head. "He's still alive, but I don't think he's going to last much longer. He won't eat and he looks so feeble. I'm not doing it right, I know I'm not."

"Oh…" Leila pulled out one of the kitchen chairs and sat down, frowning thoughtfully. "Didn't Mrs Bell say something about that? I'm sure your dad told me last night, when he didn't want any milk then."

Ellie sniffed shakily. "Yes. That sometimes they're so scared they freeze up."

"That was it." Leila rubbed Ellie's arm. "Ellie, think about it. If it's something Mrs Bell knew might happen, it's got to be pretty common, hasn't it? Maybe it even happens with all rescued hares. You're not doing anything wrong.

Why don't we give her a ring in a bit and check? We can say you're worried."

Ellie stared at Leila, her mouth slightly open. Why hadn't she thought of that? Mrs Bell had explained how important it was that only one person fed the hare, so he wasn't getting used to being around people and losing his wildness. Looking after him had felt like it had to be Ellie's special responsibility. *Maybe I listened to her too much,* Ellie thought tiredly. *I felt like I needed to do everything on my own. But of course I can ask for advice…*

"Thanks," she whispered to Leila. "I could definitely call her later, couldn't I?"

"You shouldn't have to worry about it all on your own," Leila agreed. "Want some toast? Maybe a hot chocolate?"

Ellie nodded. "Yes please."

"I could try helping you feed him, if you want?" Leila suggested, a few minutes later, when she set the toast down in front of Ellie. "Maybe it would be easier with two of us."

"You can't!" Ellie said sharply, and then she shook her head as she saw Leila flinch back. "Sorry... I didn't mean it like that. I'm not being – like I was the other day. It's because – I mean, didn't Dad tell you? – Mrs Bell said only one person must do the feeding. Honestly. It's because the leveret isn't supposed to get used to humans – it would make it harder when he's released back into the wild, you see. If he thinks humans are nice things with food."

"Oh... Yes, I see," Leila agreed, rather sadly. "Your dad did say something about that."

"And I think you might smell too much

like Biscuit," Ellie added. "Hares are really
scared of cats."

Leila looked down at herself, as if she was
surprised to think she might smell like a cat,
and Ellie giggled, reaching out to pick a ginger
hair off Leila's dressing gown. "See?"

"Oh yes, maybe…"

*That was the first time I ever touched her
on purpose,* Ellie realized, sipping her hot
chocolate.

Mrs Bell promised Ellie she hadn't done
anything wrong. She volunteered to come out
and help without Ellie even having to ask.

"Try again tonight," she told Ellie on the
phone. "If he's still not wanting to feed, I will
come round in the morning – but I don't think

it's you, Ellie. Remember what I said – he probably just needs time."

That night, Ellie got the feed ready and Leila wandered out into the garden as she headed to the summerhouse.

"I know you need to keep the doors shut," Leila murmured. "I just thought maybe someone else being in the garden might make it a bit less worrying? Especially since it's getting dark."

Ellie smiled at her gratefully and waved as she closed the summerhouse doors. It did seem to help, knowing that someone else was there. When she came closer to the cage, she saw that the hare had moved – her cardigan was squashed up against one end of the cage now, and the hare was at the other end, eyeing her cautiously.

"You moved!" Ellie whispered. She swung round, and put her thumb up to Leila, a huge grin on her face. Leila gave her a surprised smile and a thumbs up back, and Ellie crouched down to undo the cage.

"Maybe you'll want to eat something tonight. That would be good, wouldn't it? You must be so hungry by now." Ellie scooped the little hare out of the cage and set him on her lap

in the towel. Was it wishful thinking, or did he seem less frozen than he had in the morning? His ears were wiggling a little, instead of being squished flat down against his back, and his nose was wobbling more. In fact, his nose was so twitchy and sweet that it made Ellie giggle.

She picked up the syringe and gave him a hopeful look. "Just have a go," she whispered, holding the end of the syringe towards his mouth. The leveret definitely seemed more alert this evening, even though his eyes still had that sunken look. He had been shut down out of fear, but now he was paying attention to everything that was going on around him – and that included the milk. As Ellie brought the syringe closer, his ears waggled and he gave a little half hop, all tangled up in the towel.

"Yes…" Ellie breathed. "That's it, come on." This time she didn't have to jab the syringe at the leveret's mouth; he put his head forwards himself and started to nuzzle at the end, sucking at the milk that was dripping out. Ellie squeezed the plunger in just a tiny bit, to keep the milk flowing, and watched disbelievingly as the little hare gulped the milk down. It was as if he was a different creature; he seemed suddenly to have worked out that she was trying to help.

"Is that nice?" she said quietly, watching him as he stopped to make a strange sort of chewing motion – he seemed to be trying to get all the milk that had dribbled out around his mouth. Then he went back to sucking, with a very businesslike air. Every so often Ellie saw a bright pink tongue sweep round his nose and mouth to catch any drops he might have missed.

"You're very clever," she murmured to him. "And so good. Oh! I didn't weigh you, I forgot, I was so excited to try feeding you. I'll do it after. Wow, Mrs Bell was right about the towel, you're very dribbly…"

The leveret glanced sideways at her, as if he'd heard, and Ellie giggled again. "Sorry… I expect you'll get better at it. Wow, you've nearly finished. You needed that, didn't you?"

The leveret sucked at the last bit of milk in the syringe, and Ellie was sure he looked offended when suddenly it didn't work any more. She pulled the syringe away gently and looked down at him with a huge, silly grin on her face. "You did it!" Then she remembered Leila, hovering outside in the gathering darkness, and she waved the empty syringe at her, and saw her stepmum clap her hands delightedly.

Ellie lifted the leveret, ready to put him in the ice-cream tub on the scales, and then nearly dropped him as he wriggled and bounced in her hands. "Oh! Wow, you really did wake up, didn't you? OK, you're going to have to stay still in here…" She hovered her hands over the tub, ready to grab him if he made a flying leap. "You put on weight! Only a tiny bit, and I suppose that's really all the milk you just drank. But I'll write it down. Oh, you did so well." Ellie scooped him up again and popped him back into his little nest of hay. "I can't just keep saying 'you', I've got to give you a name." She watched for a moment as the little hare snuffled at the hay. "You look like a Henry." Ellie smiled to herself. "Henry Hare... See you tomorrow, Henry," she whispered, as she fixed the top of the cage back on.

She gathered everything up and hurried to open the summerhouse doors. "Leila! He drank it – all of it! I think it's going to be OK!"

When Ellie rang Mrs Bell to tell her what had happened, the old lady was delighted – but she did warn Ellie not to get too excited. Hares were still very delicate, she explained. Sometimes, even with the most experienced carers, they just didn't survive. "Not that I think anything's going to happen to Henry, Ellie. It's just I don't want you to feel as if you've done something wrong. You're being brilliant – Henry's so lucky you found him."

Over the next couple of weeks, even though Ellie couldn't stop worrying about Henry, and all the things that might go wrong, she still loved caring for him. He was so happy now whenever she came to feed him. Early in the morning when she wandered down the garden feeling sleepy and dazed, seeing a tiny hare bouncing excitedly inside his cage was the nicest way to wake up. Ellie felt so lucky watching him sucking and slurping at the syringe of milk, his nose blissfully twitching as he nestled in the towel on her lap.

But every so often, Ellie would remember that she was only caring for Henry so he could go back to his wild life on the common. She knew it was for the best, of course, but it was so hard to imagine Henry not being at home. Running her fingers over his soft fur and velvet ears as he drank his milk, she couldn't think how it would be without him.

Henry was getting bigger. He was starting to look more like a hare – his ears were longer, and so were his legs. Dad said he looked like a teenage boy, legs everywhere. He was having dry food pellets as well as milk now, and Ellie went hunting for wildflowers on the common to feed him. He loved dandelions, the leaves but especially the bright yellow flowers. He ate as many as Ellie could find, and she took some brilliant photos of him eating them, with a fluffy yellow-petal moustache sticking out. He loved the freedom of the big garden run that Mrs Bell had brought round, and he was starting to nibble at the fresh grass for himself now.

He was like a different creature, Ellie thought, watching him hop around the run and enthusiastically seize a mouthful of grass. But in only a few weeks' time, Henry would be gone.

9

Ellie walked down the garden, her arms laden
with the scales, Henry's milk, his dry food
pellets, a handful of white clover which she
and Ruby had picked on the common that
afternoon, and her towel – Henry hadn't got any
tidier about drinking his milk.

She nearly dropped the lot when she found
Biscuit perched on top of Henry's wire run,
peering through the mesh and practically
licking his lips. There was no sign of Henry,
thankfully – *he must be in the little covered
hutch at the end of his run,* Ellie thought.

"Biscuit! What are you doing out here?" Ellie hurriedly set down the pile and went to grab the runaway cat, but Biscuit had other ideas. He leaped off the run and scooted away, leading Ellie on a chase around the garden, darting into flower beds and under bushes, until finally she caught him as he

tried to jump and scrabble
his way up the apple tree.
Ellie grabbed him round the
middle and carefully unhooked
his claws from the tree bark,
then she dashed back up the
garden with Biscuit squirming
in her arms.

She shoved Biscuit at Leila, who was cooking the tea and gaped at her in surprise as Ellie stuffed the cat into her arms and then raced back out into the garden. Henry had been inside the little hutch, but Mrs Bell had told her that hares were very sensitive to stress, and they had an amazing sense of smell. Biscuit hadn't been able to get inside the run, but what if he'd managed to terrify Henry just by staring at him? Henry might have gone back into that awful frozen state he'd been in when she first found him. Or perhaps Henry had retreated into the hutch after Biscuit had swiped at him with his claws!

Ellie stopped by the run, panicked and panting, and peered in. Henry gazed back at her through the wire, looking faintly surprised. There was a bit of grass hanging out of the corner of his mouth.

"You're all right," Ellie said thankfully. "Did

you even know Biscuit was there? You don't look very worried."

Henry mumbled the grass into his mouth and then went back to nibbling his way around the run. He seemed not to have noticed Biscuit at all. Ellie heaved a huge sigh that seemed to go all the way down to the bottom of her stomach, and then swung round and marched back into the house.

"You need to be more careful about Biscuit!" she told Leila, glowering at her.

"But where was he?" Leila asked.

"Climbing on top of Henry's run."

"Oh no. I'm really sorry, Ellie. Is Henry all right? Biscuit didn't hurt him?"

"He's fine," Ellie admitted grudgingly. "But he might not have been! Biscuit was on top of the run looking in through the wire – he was obviously trying to get at Henry."

"Oh dear…" Leila murmured.

"He could have eaten him!"

"I don't think he could get inside the run, surely?" Leila said.

"Maybe not – but he could still scare Henry to death. I mean it! Mrs Bell said that hares get stressed really easily, so stressed they could even die."

"I'm so sorry, Ellie. I don't know how Biscuit got out – I'll keep a closer watch on him in future."

"If Biscuit hurts Henry I'll never forgive him," Ellie growled. "Or you."

Leila pulled out one of the kitchen chairs from the table with a nasty screech, and sat down on it hard. Then she looked up at Ellie, who was still glaring. "That might be tricky, since you already can't forgive me for marrying your dad."

Ellie opened her mouth, and then shut it again, and just stood staring at her stepmum. Leila never said things like that. Never. She just smiled nicely and sadly and put up with every unpleasant thing Ellie said.

Leila shrugged. "I can understand it's difficult. But it would be nice if you gave me a chance."

"I – I have," Ellie stammered.

Leila looked up at her thoughtfully and then shook her head. "No. I really don't think so.

I wouldn't be happy if I thought someone had come along to try and replace my mum either, but I've tried very hard to show you I didn't want to do that."

Ellie couldn't find a single thing to say. She just gaped at Leila. Dad had sat down with her for so many "talks" about Mum, and about how marrying Leila didn't mean he was forgetting her, and how he never expected Leila to replace Ellie's mum. But Leila had never talked to Ellie about it. They didn't often talk at all.

"I'll make sure I keep more of an eye on Biscuit, OK? Now hadn't you better go and get Henry indoors and feed him? He'll be getting chilly."

Ellie just nodded and slipped back out of the kitchen. She really didn't know what to say. Had she been that unfair? She supposed it wasn't actually Leila's fault that she'd fallen in love with Ellie's dad...

Ellie picked up all the stuff from where she'd dropped it on the lawn. Henry's milk probably wasn't warm any more – she hoped he wouldn't mind. She laid everything out on the little table in the summerhouse and then went back to collect the leveret. It was a good system, bringing him in to have his milk. Henry needed to sleep indoors, because the nights were still chilly, and because he needed to be safe from foxes, but he liked the garden run so much more than his cage. Ellie was pretty sure he'd be a lot harder to catch if he didn't know he was about to be fed. As it was, he gave a couple of springy little hops around the run, but then let Ellie grab him pretty easily. He snuggled up against her cardigan, snuffling around as if he thought she might have the milk syringe hidden inside it somewhere.

"Come on then," Ellie murmured to him. She was still turning the talk with Leila over and over in her head – and remembering the time a few weeks back, when Leila had been so helpful when Henry wouldn't eat. *Did*

I even say thank you? Ellie wondered. She couldn't remember, and that probably meant she hadn't.

"We have to weigh you before you can have that," Ellie said, half laughing as Henry tried to scramble towards the syringe. "Hold still, Henry... Oh, wow. Five hundred and fifty-two grams, that's huge! Sorry, but it means you won't be getting milk for much longer, mate. I think it might be solid food only now. I'll have to find you a lot more dandelions. Ruby said she could bring some from her garden too." She lifted the leveret on to her lap, and let him suck greedily at the milk. "Mrs Bell's going to be so pleased with you. She's coming to see how you are tomorrow. I'll be able to tell her about all the weight you've put on, and ask her about stopping your milk." Ellie stroked her hand gently over Henry's ears.

"You're nearly five times the size you were when I found you," she whispered. "You were my tiny little scared baby, and now look at you…"

Henry stopped sucking for a moment to glance at her, and then slurped down the rest of his milk in seconds.

Mrs Bell crouched down by Henry's run, watching him devour the pile of clover flowers that Ellie had dropped in for him. "He's fantastic," she told Ellie and her dad, smiling. "I can't believe how big and healthy he looks. You've done amazingly with him, Ellie." Mrs Bell nodded. "If anyone brings me a hare again, I'm going to be straight on the phone to you – you're more of an expert than I am now, you realize?"

Ellie ducked her head shyly. She couldn't imagine rearing another hare – although she thought that Mrs Bell was probably quite hard to say no to. But all her love and everything she'd learned belonged to Henry.

"So, did you say he was five hundred and fifty grams now?" Mrs Bell asked.

"Five hundred and fifty-two," Ellie said proudly.

"That's amazing." Mrs Bell straightened up

with a little wheeze. "You're right, I think
he's definitely big enough to be on solid
food only now – and you should be able to
release him back on to the common in a
couple of weeks."

"Wow! You mean, Ellie's done it?" Dad
said. "That's fantastic!"

Ellie tried hard to smile. It was fantastic. It
was what they had been aiming for all along.
So why did she feel as though the bottom
had just dropped out of her stomach?

The two weeks left with Henry seemed to
disappear, however hard Ellie tried to hold on
to them. She took more and more photos, and
tried to spend as much time as she could in
the garden, watching Henry hop about in his

run. He didn't know he was going, of course. Would he mind? Ellie wasn't sure.

The next Sunday afternoon, Ellie was doing her science homework lying on the grass next to Henry's run. If she had to give him up in one more week, she didn't want to miss any of the time she could have with him.

"Hey, Ellie…"

Ellie rolled over to see Leila looking down at her. She held out a plate with some cookies on it. "Would you like one? I just made them."

"Oh… Thanks."

"I noticed you didn't eat very much at lunchtime."

Ellie gave her a surprised look. She wasn't used to Leila noticing that sort of thing. Or at least noticing it and saying something about it. Maybe her stepmum always had noticed, but she hadn't felt as though she was allowed to say. "I wasn't very hungry…"

"Your dad told me about what Mrs Bell said last weekend. He was pleased. I think he's looking forward to his lawn looking perfect again."

Ellie snorted. "Henry mows the lawn for him now."

"Mmmm. Perhaps we should get a little goat. I've always liked them. Not sure I could convince your dad, though." They were silent for a moment and then Leila added, "Ellie, are you OK about Henry going?"

"I always knew he was going back to the wild," Ellie muttered. "That was the whole point."

"I know. It doesn't mean it's easy when it

happens, though. You've spent so much time looking after him – and worrying about him."

Ellie sniffed and looked at the run so she didn't have to look at Leila. Henry was sitting in the middle of it with a clover flower drooping out the corner of his mouth. It made him look a bit dopey.

"He makes me think of my mum," she whispered.

"Oh… Why?"

"We used to sit on the bench in front of the house, and we saw hares together. A few times. That was when she was really ill, in the spring before she died. That's why I got so excited about seeing them again. I hadn't noticed them, not any of the years in between. It felt so special. And Mum would have loved looking after Henry. She really would."

"She would have been very proud of you, taking care of him," Leila said gently. "You do know that, don't you? And you know how proud your dad is? He's told everyone at work about you and your hare."

Ellie sniffed again, but she found she was smiling. She hadn't known that. It was nice to think of Dad being proud. "Oh…" she murmured, watching Henry chew through another big mouthful of clover.

"Don't forget your cookie."

Ellie watched Leila walk back into the house and then she bit into the cookie, feeling the chocolate melt in her mouth. Leila actually made very good cookies, she thought, as she took another bite. Possibly even better than her mum's. And it was OK to think that.

10

"What are you going to put him in, to take him to the common?" Dad asked. "Mrs Bell took the carrier back home with her, didn't she?"

Ellie nodded. "I hadn't thought of that – I mean, maybe I could just carry him out there? But that's probably not a good idea. I haven't touched him much at all this week – I didn't want him to smell of me when he went back outside."

Sophie smiled at her. "Awww. In case the others think he's not a proper hare?"

"Sort of... I know it sounds silly..."

"No, I think that's very sensible," Dad agreed.

Ellie sighed to herself. It was sensible, she knew it was, but it had been so hard. Henry had been eating only solid food since Mrs Bell had come to see him – and he hadn't liked that at all, not for the first couple of days. He'd expected his milk at bedtime, and he'd been very confused when Ellie didn't feed him. He sat in the cage looking outraged, that first night. Ellie was sure he was glaring at her. Now she had to tempt him out of his garden run with something really delicious, like a whole handful of dandelion flowers, or a bit off one of Dad's parsley plants.

Because Henry wasn't having milk any

more, Ellie hadn't needed to cuddle him close to feed him – she only had to lift him from the cage to the run and back again, that was all. She'd stopped snuggling him, she just held him round the middle under his front paws, and popped him in and out.

She hated it.

"I suppose I could just put him in a cardboard box with lots of hay," Ellie suggested. "It isn't for very long. And there are some boxes in the utility room."

"When are you going to do it?" Leila asked.

Ellie stared down at her cereal and shrugged. "After breakfast, I suppose. There's no point waiting, is there?" She knew her voice sounded hard and don't-care-ish, but she couldn't help it. If she thought too much about what she was going to do, she would cry. "He probably needs some time outside to get used to things before it gets dark. You could come and help, if you like," she muttered ungraciously to Leila.

She didn't see Dad and Sophie exchanging a shocked look, but she could hear the smile in Leila's voice when she said, "Oh... Yes. That would be great. Shout for me when you're ready."

Ellie went to find a box after breakfast – Dad didn't like throwing things away, and boxes were useful. She found a good solid one that looked about the same size as the carrier Mrs Bell had lent them – but of course Henry was so much bigger now. Ellie looked at it doubtfully. He was only going to be in it for about five minutes, she decided.

It would be OK. She backed into the kitchen holding it, and held it out to Leila.

"Do you think that's big enough?"

Leila nodded, and they went out to the summerhouse to fetch the hay. "I won't need any of this after today," Ellie said in a small voice, looking at all the cluttery bits of leveret equipment that had ended up in there. "I suppose we'll just give it back to Mrs Bell."

"I know you can't imagine wanting to rear another leveret," Leila said. "But maybe you'll feel differently in a little while. Mrs Bell was right when she said you're an expert now. I looked it up online, and everyone says how difficult it is to hand rear a hare successfully. You'll probably get people wanting to send you baby leverets from all over the county!"

Ellie half sniffed, half laughed. "Maybe. It won't be the same, though."

Leila patted her arm gently. "No. I know it won't. But think how happy Henry will be, back out on the common."

"Yes." Ellie nodded firmly. "Can you hold that bag of hay open for me?" She stuffed the box with great handfuls of the sweet-smelling hay until it was half full and looked comfy. "OK then. Let's go and get him."

They went out to open the run, and Henry came loping curiously towards them. It wasn't the time of day for Ellie to put him back in the summerhouse and he knew it.

"Oh, Henry," Ellie said sadly. She opened the top of the run and Henry whipped round and darted into the little hutch at the end. "He thinks I'm going to put him indoors." Ellie sighed. "Hang on, I'll go and nick a bit more of Dad's parsley."

"He likes *parsley*?" Leila asked, laughing.

"Yes, it's his favourite, but don't tell Dad, please. I don't think he'd want it being fed to a hare – he grew it from seed..." Ellie came back with a little handful of fresh green parsley, and she reached down into the run, holding it out for the leveret. "Look,

Henry ... parsley... You looooove parsley,
come on..."

Henry appeared at the door of the hutch,
eyeing her suspiciously – but also eyeing the
parsley. Ellie's stomach twisted as she saw
his nose wriggle. She loved his nose, the way
it wobbled about all the time – she didn't
think any other animals had noses like that,
unless maybe elephants counted.

Henry hopped towards her and delicately lipped the parsley out of her hand. Ellie scooped him up while he was still chewing and popped him into the cardboard box, quickly folding down the flaps at the top.

There was a short moment of silence, and Ellie was just about to pick the box up, when suddenly an eerie, terrified scream echoed out. Ellie jumped back, and then squeaked as the box started to rock about. There were loud thumps too – Henry had to be kicking the inside of the box.

"What is it?" Leila gasped. "What's wrong with him?"

"I don't know!" Ellie stared at the box, but Henry was still screaming. She couldn't leave him in there like that. She wrenched the flaps open and grabbed him out, dropping him quickly back into the run.

"Ellie, what happened?" Leila whispered,
watching Henry hop
shakily across the
run to hide in
the hutch.

Ellie shook
her head,
looking at
the empty box
and biting her lip.
What had upset him
so much? "Maybe it was too small?" she
suggested, peering worriedly into the run.
She could just see Henry, huddled inside the
hutch. "Oh... Oh, it was dark." She looked
up at Leila. "I don't think he liked being
shut up in a small, dark space. He hasn't

been in anything as small as the pet carrier for weeks and weeks. Hares always live in open spaces, they don't sleep in burrows or anything like that. Small and dark doesn't feel safe to them like it would to a rabbit."

"What could we put him in instead?" Leila asked, frowning. "His night-time cage isn't that big, is it? Could we get him to go in there, and then take the top off when we get out on to the common?"

"Yes! Oh, that's brilliant. He won't be scared of the cage, will he? I mean, he doesn't like it that much, but only because it's smaller than his run. Thanks, Leila." Ellie reached out and hugged Leila tightly, and then let go, feeling embarrassed. She thought Leila was probably embarrassed too. She didn't seem to know what to say.

"Shall I – um... I could get the cage out... Or do you think we ought to let him calm down a bit?"

Ellie nodded. "Maybe we can try again in an hour or so? I'm going to go and pick him some dandelions, I can't keep stealing parsley – Dad's going to notice."

An hour later, Ellie and Leila crept back
to look at Henry. He didn't seem to have
remembered the scary box, instead he looked
hopefully at Ellie, clearly expecting her to
have brought him some delicious treat. He
wriggled a bit when she picked him up
out of the run, but he didn't seem worried
about being put in his cage, even though it
was unusual for it to be on the grass. He
just peered out curiously through the wire,
looking around as Ellie and Leila lifted up
the cage.

"There's a door in the side that I don't use
much," Ellie said, as they negotiated their
way round to the front of the house. "We
can open that and then he can just take
his time."

"Uh-huh," Leila agreed, hitching the cage

up a bit. "This is heavier than I thought it would be. How far are we going?"

"I thought over by that clump of bramble bushes – not far from the house," Ellie explained. "I don't know where his mother left him, you see, because the fox could have carried him for ages. But if we let him go by the brambles he's got long grass to hide in, and the bushes too if he wants."

They bumped carefully over the long grass, holding the cage sideways between them, with Henry gazing out across the grassland. He looked fascinated, Ellie thought. She wondered if he remembered anything from his life out on the common before.

Eventually they came level with the bramble clump, and set the cage down. Ellie looked around worriedly. "It's nothing like

it was when I found him," she murmured.
"The grass is so long, and all the wildflowers
are out now. Maybe he won't know what
to do."

"He'll love it, Ellie," Leila said, smiling at
the view. "Look, there's so much space. And
it isn't far to the trees over there if he wants
something more sheltered. He showed you this
morning that he hated being shut in, didn't
he?"

"I suppose," Ellie agreed reluctantly. She
crouched down by the cage and opened
the side door, hooking it right back so that
Henry could see he was free to hop out.
"We'd better go back a bit," she whispered to
Leila, and they retreated a few steps, sitting
down in the long grass to watch.

"I wonder if he understands he can get out,"

Leila murmured. "Oh! Oh, wow, look at him!"

Henry definitely understood that the door was open. He looked out of it for a couple of seconds, and then jumped on to the grass. He crouched by the cage, and then hopped forwards – and again. That was as far as he'd ever been able to go in the run, Ellie realized. He was just getting used to having all that space.

All of a sudden he set off again, racing across the meadow in long, leaping bounds. For the first time Ellie could properly see the white of his tail. She'd never seen him move fast enough for the black top to bounce up and show the white underneath.

He belongs out here, Ellie thought.

But it didn't make it any easier to watch him race away.

Ellie looked at the time on her phone, and
nibbled her bottom lip. If she was quick…
She turned off the path back to the house and
headed up to the highest part of the common,
where the best view was. Where her mum's
bench was.

Before she sat down she stood looking
at it for a few moments, reading the little
message over and over again. *Remembering
Molly.*

She did remember, she just wished that she
remembered *more*.

"We let him go, Mum…" she said out loud.
"On Saturday. It was so weird this morning, I
got up to go and put him in his run, and I was
nearly dressed and trying to hurry, and then I

remembered that I didn't have him any more. It was horrible." She leaned back against the bench and sighed. "You'd have loved him…"

Ellie wasn't sure what made her look up – whether she actually heard something, or it was some strange other sense that told her. But there in front of her, just a little way down the slope, was a hare. The sun was lighting up his tawny-brown coat, and his eyes glittered amber. He was looking at her.

"Henry?" Ellie whispered. She wasn't sure. The hare was quite small, and it had the same beautiful dark ear-tips that Henry had – but all hares had dark ears…

The hare hopped a little closer and stared at her, as if he was thinking.

"It *is* you…" Ellie felt her face curve into a smile. "Oh, Henry. Mum, it's Henry…"

The hare watched her a moment longer and then turned to hop slowly away across the slope, stopping every so often to nibble the grass and then look around, alert and tall, his ears twitching. He looked so at home, as if he was right where he was meant to be.

Ellie watched him until he disappeared behind a little stand of trees, and then she wandered home, still smiling, to find Leila in the kitchen, making a cup of tea.

"You look a bit dazed, are you OK?"

Ellie nodded. "I saw him." She laughed. She couldn't help it; happiness was bubbling up inside her. Henry was all right! And he knew her, he'd come back to see her. Maybe even to tell her that everything was fine.

"Henry?" Leila set her mug down, smiling. "Really? Oh, Ellie, that's amazing, how did he look?"

"He was wonderful," Ellie murmured. "He looked perfect." She smiled hopefully at Leila. "Are you busy?"

"No, not really."

"Do you want to come and sit outside for a bit?" Ellie suggested. "We might see him again."

Leila nodded. "Good idea. I'll bring my tea." She followed Ellie out to the bench at the front of the house, and they gazed over the wildmeadow, listening to the wind sighing in the long grass. Leila sipped her tea, and whispered, "This is beautiful, even if we don't see any hares."

"It is." Ellie sighed happily and leaned against Leila's shoulder, watching for dark ears dancing above the grass.

The Hideaway Deer

From best-selling author
HOLLY WEBB

When Lola moves house she can't help
worrying about leaving her old life behind.
There are some good things, though. She
loves her home with its huge, rambling
garden and the deer that sometimes
wander in through the broken fence.

Then one day Lola comes across
a fawn who seems to be in trouble.
She's determined to do everything she
can to help the terrified little deer, but
will she be able to do it on her own?

THE

SILVER

PONY

From international
best-selling author

HOLLY WEBB

Daisy loves watching the ponies
that wander wild through the woods
near her home. They're beautiful but
she's always been afraid to get too close.

Then one day, to Daisy's amazement,
a pretty silvery-white pony approaches her.
Can it tell how much Daisy needs a friend?

HOLLY WEBB

Holly Webb started out as a children's book editor and wrote her first series for the publisher she worked for. She has been writing ever since, with over one hundred books to her name. Holly lives in Berkshire, with her husband and three children. Holly's pet cats are always nosying around when she is trying to type on her laptop.

For more information about Holly Webb visit:

www.holly-webb.com